Honey Bear
Finds a Friend

By Alice Popper
Illustrated by Oliver Orville

For Marissa, my very own Princess Honey,
and for my special little friend, Ben —A.P.

MERRIGOLD PRESS • NEW YORK

Once there was a sweet little bear named Marissa. And because she was so sweet, everyone called her Honey. She lived with her mother and father and brother, Ben, in the forest.

She had a favorite toy. It was her teddy bear. Honey never went anywhere without her teddy.

When she played "tea party," her teddy was an invited guest, along with her dolls.

When Honey rode on the swing, she would
hold her teddy tightly so he would not fall off.

When Honey built castles in the sandbox, she would sit her teddy beside her. "Here, Tiny Teddy, I'll fill your pail with sand. You're much too little to fill it yourself," she would say.

When Honey went splashing in her wading pool, she always placed Tiny Teddy at the edge so he could watch.

And at bedtime Honey would snuggle with
Tiny Teddy under the cozy blanket. Then she
would kiss him most tenderly and whisper,
"Good night. Sweet dreams."

One hot summer afternoon Honey was playing in the garden. She was having a "dress-up party" with Tiny Teddy. With some bits of lacy curtains, a gold-thread veil, and a paper crown, Honey made herself into a princess. And she made Tiny Teddy the royal crown prince baby.

Honey was pretending the trees were her royal castle's courtyard. A rock was her throne, and a pine tree branch was the crown prince baby's cradle. Princess Honey was singing a lullaby to her baby.

Honey was so involved in her game that she didn't notice that the wind had started to blow. She didn't notice the birds screeching in alarm. She didn't notice the squirrels skittering this way and that.

When she heard a faint rumbling in the distance, she looked up for an instant and saw a big fearsome-looking cloud monster gulping up the blue sky. It was getting darker and darker among the pine trees, but Honey continued her game.

Then suddenly thunder cracked and the clouds
burst open. A torrent of rain came crashing down.
Honey dashed from the trees, seeking shelter.
"Honey, Honey," Mother called from the
porch. "Come inside, this minute!"
Honey ran toward the house.

"Just look at the rain," said Mother. "And you still out here playing."

Honey was glad to be inside where it was safe and warm.

It rained for a long time, a big, loud, slopping rain that dug pools in the flower beds and made the tree limbs hang low and heavy.

When the downpour finally stopped, Honey announced, "Now Tiny Teddy and I can go back to our castle."

She looked around. "Where is my teddy? Where is he?" she cried.

"Maybe you left him outside," suggested Ben Bear.

"Outside? In that terrible storm. How could I forget Tiny Teddy?" wailed Honey.

"Don't cry," said Ben. "He'll be fine. Let's go find him."

Honey and Ben ran outside. They looked around the dripping trees of the royal courtyard. No Tiny Teddy.

They peered under the swing. No teddy.

They searched in the sandbox.
No teddy bear.

They looked in the wading
pool. "My teddy is gone,"
wailed Honey. "He was angry
with me and he ran away."

Ben patted Honey on the head. "You know he couldn't run away. He's just a toy."

"Not to me he isn't. He's my teddy!" said Honey, ready to cry.

Now Mother and Father joined the search.

It was getting dark, and the evening fog was rising from the damp, mossy ground. Honey was crying.

"Let's go inside, little one. We'll find Tiny Teddy tomorrow," Mother suggested softly.

Suddenly Honey heard something. "What was that?" she said.

Everyone stood still and listened. Then they heard a small whimpering sound coming from under the porch.

"Something is under there," cried Ben, already down on his knees. Ben and Honey crouched low and peered under the porch.

"Oh, look, a puppy!" cried Honey.

A tiny wet and bedraggled puppy was cowering in a corner. It was snuggled up close against Tiny Teddy.

"There's Tiny Teddy!" screamed Honey Bear.
"The puppy must have stolen him!"

"No, he didn't," said Ben Bear. "He made
friends with your teddy in the storm and carried
him to safety."

Ben Bear tried to coax the shivering puppy from his hiding place. But the puppy refused to budge.

"Poor little thing," said Mother. "He looks so scared. I bet he is lost."

"I guess we could give him a home," said Father.

"Don't be scared, little puppy," said Honey Bear softly. At the sound of her voice the puppy picked up his head and crawled over to Honey, carrying the teddy in his mouth. Honey Bear put her arms around both of them and hugged them tight.

"Thank you, little puppy," said Honey Bear. "Thank you for taking care of my teddy. Now we can all be friends and play together."

And so the little lost puppy found a home, and Honey Bear had both her teddy and a puppy to cuddle and love.